MANDIE AND MOLLIE
& THE ANGEL'S VISIT

ĝ©ĝ©ĝ©ĝ©ĝ©ĝ©ĝ©ĝ©ĝ©ĝ©ĝ©

LOIS GLADYS LEPPARD

Mandie® Mysteries

R4.8/2.0pt.   +48356

DATE DUE

FOLLETT

MANDIE AND MOLLIE
& THE ANGEL'S VISIT

LOIS GLADYS LEPPARD

BETHANYHOUSE
MINNEAPOLIS, MINNESOTA

Mandie and Mollie & the Angel's Visit
Copyright © 1998
Lois Gladys Leppard

MANDIE® is registered trademark of Lois Gladys Leppard

Cover and text illustrations by Chris Wold Dyrud

Published by Bethany House Publishers
A Ministry of Bethany Fellowship Internationa
11300 Hampshire Avenue South
Minneapolis, Minnesota 55438

Printed in the United States of America

Library of Congress Cataloging-in-Publication Data

Leppard, Lois Gladys.
    Mandie and Mollie—the angel's visit / by Lois Gladys Leppard.
        p.   cm.
    Summary: Thirteen-year-old Mandie and her friends and family help the young Irish orphan Mollie look for her aunt, while Mollie learns about Jesus and persistently looks for angels.
        ISBN 1–55661–648–1 (pbk.)
        ISBN 0–7642–2063–2
        [1. Orphans—Fiction. 2. Irish Americans—Fiction.
3. Angels—Fiction.] 4. Christian life—Fiction. I. Title.
PZ7.L556Macr   1998
[Fic]—dc21   97–45479
                                                              CIP
                                                              AC

For
Steve Oates
Dear Friend of Mandie,
and
in Memory of
Winslow,
RIP

LOIS GLADYS LEPPARD has been a professional singer/actress/playwright. She and her two sisters, Sibyl and Louise, sang professionally as the Larke Sisters in New York. The group starred in the operetta *Bohemian Girl* and were presented at Carnegie Hall, among other presentations. She studied at the New York School of Music and at the Voice Beautiful Institute in New York under Glenn Morris Starkie, who had been a student of Enrico Caruso.

As a drama student, she was in the group that organized the present Little Theatre in her hometown. She has written several plays and was at one time with Columbia Pictures. She wrote and had published a song at the age of fifteen.

Contents

Mandie and Mollie
& the Angel's Visit
A Drama in Three Acts

Part One

"Mandie Shaw, do ye be havin' leprechauns in this place where ye live?" Mollie asked as soon as she stepped inside the Shaw house. She darted ahead of the others down the hallway and quickly peered into the parlor.

"Let's take off your cape, Mollie," Mandie said, catching up with her and stopping to remove the garment.

"We'll be back down shortly, dear," Elizabeth, Mandie's mother, called to her as she led Jane Hamilton on toward the staircase.

Celia Hamilton, Mandie's longtime friend and roommate at school in Asheville, North Carolina, hung her coat and tam on the hall tree and joined Mandie and Mollie as they went into the parlor.

"Celia, I'm so glad you and your mother could come

9

and spend the Easter holidays with us," Mandie told her. They sat down and Mollie roamed about the room. "And that you could bring Mollie, too. I do believe she has grown a couple of inches since we brought her home with us from Ireland."

"She is growing fast," Celia agreed. "And she also gets around fast, you'll find out."

Mollie, after inspecting everything in the room, finally came to stand by the fireplace, where the fire was crackling brightly. "Mandie, ye niver told me. Do ye be havin' leprechauns around here?" She frowned as she looked at Mandie with her bright blue eyes and pushed a carrot-red lock of hair back from her face.

Mandie sighed and said, "Oh, Mollie, are you still chasing leprechauns? I don't believe we have any in this house, or in this town, in fact."

The little ten-year-old girl walked up closer to Mandie and said, "But there might be one here some place. I'll be lookin' and watchin' for one while I be stayin' here with ye."

"But you don't need to find a leprechaun now to get his pot of gold," Mandie reminded her. "You have a nice home with Celia."

"When Celia finds me aunt, the lady may be needin' the gold," the girl said.

"We may never find your aunt, Mollie," Celia told her. "So far the detectives my mother has had looking for her haven't found any trace of her, so you may have to live with us until you grow up."

Mollie looked at Celia thoughtfully and said, "I still be lookin' for a leprechaun."

Snowball, Mandie's white cat, wandered into the

room right then and Mollie quickly grabbed him and picked him up. She took him over to a stool, sat down, and began talking to him as she stroked his fur. "I know ye. Yer name be Snowball, and ye came to Ireland with Mandie last summer."

Mandie asked Celia in a low voice, "Is your mother still trying to find Mollie's aunt, or has she given up?"

"No, she hasn't given up, but so far no one has found a trace of her," Celia replied. "Remember the police authorities in Ireland told your grandmother that the aunt had come to the United States when Mollie was a baby, so that's a long time ago."

"But they also told us the aunt was last heard from somewhere in Virginia," Mandie said. "Of course she might have moved on to another part of the country after that." Then lowering her voice to a whisper she asked, "Does your mother plan to keep Mollie if she never locates the aunt?"

"I think so," Celia whispered back. "She is quite a handful, never having had any discipline in Ireland and being allowed to roam the streets there, but Aunt Rebecca has become attached to her, and I sorta think she hopes we never find her aunt so she can keep Mollie."

"How is your aunt Rebecca doing in trying to educate her?" Mandie asked.

"Well, you know Aunt Rebecca used to be a schoolteacher, and this gives her something to do," Celia said with a big smile.

"Have y'all heard anything more about Mrs. Wiley, the woman who was keeping Mollie in Ireland?" Mandie asked.

"Yes, Mother stays in touch with her," Celia replied.

"I'm sure Mother sends her money, too. The woman is in such bad shape now—after that accident she had and no one to support her. Even though she is in that rest home for the poor in Belfast, she does need some money."

Mandie rubbed her arms and said, "It still gives me goose bumps just thinking about that awful fire. I'm so thankful we were able to save Mollie and Mrs. Wiley, although the lady did get seriously injured."

"I know," Celia agreed. "Never in all my thirteen years have I been so frightened."

Mandie happened to glance at the door. Liza was standing there staring through the doorway at Mollie. Mandie called to her, "Come on in, Liza. This is Mollie." When the little girl looked up, she added, "And, Mollie, this is Liza."

Mollie instantly jumped up and ran to the young maid. She dropped the cat in her haste. He meowed loudly and ran out the door. "Do ye be knowin' if there be leprechauns in this house?" she asked.

"Be whut?" Liza asked, frowning as she looked at the little girl and then at Mandie. "Missy 'Manda, dat lil' girl she don't speak good English."

Mandie and Celia both smiled. Mollie stood there,

looking up at Liza and waiting for her answer.

"She wants to know if we have leprechauns in this house," Mandie explained.

"If we has whut?" Liza asked, puzzled.

"Leprechauns," Mandie replied, and then with a big sigh she explained. "You have probably never heard of leprechauns. You see, some people in Ireland believe they exist. And Mollie is always looking for one because they are supposed to own a pot of gold."

"Pot o' gold?" Liza asked, her black eyes widening.

Celia looked at Mandie and said, "You might as well explain what this is all about."

"Yes," Mandie agreed. "Liza, many, many years ago these leprechauns were supposed to live in Ireland. The English, or American, name for them is shoemaker—"

"Like dat shoemaker man named Pat whut works down in dat shop on Main Street?" Liza excitedly interrupted. "But he ain't got no pot o' gold."

Mollie was listening and now she became excited, too. "Ye know where there be a leprechaun? Show me where he be."

"No, no, no!" Mandie said loudly to stop their conversation. "No, Liza. Pat is a shoemaker, but he's not a leprechaun. Maybe leprechauns only lived in Ireland. We don't have any here."

Mollie grasped Liza's hand and said, "Will ye take me to see this Pat shoemaker? Please, I say."

Liza looked from Mollie to Mandie and then back to Mollie and said, "But Missy 'Manda she say dis heah Pat he ain't de right kind o' lepcawn, or whatever you calls it. And he sho ain't got no pot o' gold. Now iffen dat's all you lookin' fo', why don't you find de end to de rainbow? Dey say it's a pot o' gold at de end."

"Do ye be knowin' where this rainbow be?" Mollie asked.

"Liza!" Mandie spoke sharply to the girl. "Please don't put such nonsensical ideas into Mollie's head. You know very well there is no pot of gold at the end of the rainbow, which I know you must have learned in church." Turning to Mollie she said, "The rainbow is God's promise to us, all of us here on earth, that the earth will never again be destroyed by water. He gave the promise to Noah after the flood was over."

Mollie looked at her in surprise for a moment and then she asked, "But how do ye be knowin' all this?"

"Because it's all in the Bible," Mandie replied. She looked at Celia and asked, "Y'all have been teaching her the Bible, haven't you?"

"Of course, Mandie," Celia said. "But there is so much she doesn't know that it's going to take a lot of time for her to understand everything."

"Anyhow, kin we find a rainbow?" Mollie asked Liza, who was still standing there with bowed head after Mandie's outburst.

"Missy 'Manda, she be right 'bout rainbows," Liza told the little girl. "Ain't no pot o' gold at de end. Dat's jes' ole tales." Then turning to look at Mandie, she said, "I'se sorry for all de tomfoolery, Missy 'Manda. 'Course I knows bettuh. Aunt Lou she tell me all 'bout rainbows long time ago."

Mollie quickly pulled on Liza's arm to get her attention and asked, "Kin we find a rainbow? Please, I say."

Mandie looked at Liza and said, "You are forgiven this time, Liza, but please remember that Mollie is young and doesn't know everything you've been taught. In fact, you could help us teach her what Easter is all about while she's here."

Liza looked at Mandie with widened eyes as she replied, "Missy 'Manda, I don't be knowin' how to teach nobody nuthin'. Y'all be needin' Aunt Lou to do de teachin'."

Mandie smiled at the young girl who was not much older than her own thirteen years and said, "That's a good idea, Liza. We'll ask Aunt Lou to help explain things to Mollie."

Mollie suddenly asked loudly, "Kin we find a rainbow? Kin we?" She looked up at Liza and then at Mandie.

"All right, Mollie, if a rainbow comes into the sky while you are here, we'll be sure to show it to you," Mandie said. "You see, we can't just make rainbows whenever we want one. God puts them in the sky usually when the sun comes out after it rains."

"We kin look for leprechauns then," Mollie decided. "Maybe they don't be made by God."

Celia had been listening to the conversation and now she said, "Mollie, God made this earth and everything in it. So if there is such a thing as a leprechaun, I'm sure God made it, too. However, I don't believe He made any leprechauns, because if He did, sooner or later you'd be able to find one."

Mollie frowned and stomped both her feet as she said angrily, "Then I be wantin' to go back to Ireland, where God didn't make everythin'."

"And I'se got to go back to de kitchen 'fo Aunt Lou

start lookin' fo' me," Liza said, quickly leaving the room.

Mandie and Celia looked at each other in dismay.

"So far only Aunt Rebecca has been able to get through to her," Celia remarked.

Mollie suddenly sat down on the floor and asked, "Where be Grandmither? She took me to this United States. Now I be wantin' Grandmither to take me back to Belfast. That I do."

"Oh, Mollie, we love you, and we don't want you to go back to Belfast," Mandie said, slipping out of her chair and sitting on the floor next to the little girl as she put an arm around her. Mollie had claimed Mandie's grandmother for her own when she brought her to the United States. "Grandmother will be coming later this week, but we don't want her to take you back to Ireland. Remember the cold place in the cellar where you lived? And lots of times you didn't have enough to eat. We want you to stay in the United States so we can take care of you, at least until we can locate your aunt." She reached to smooth Mollie's carrot-red hair, but the little girl pulled away from her.

"But I might be findin' a leprechaun in Ireland, and then I could git his pot o' gold, and I could be gittin' me a new home to stay in, that I could," Mollie told her.

Celia joined them on the floor as she said, "Mollie, have you ever thought about the fact that if you did find a leprechaun and he had a pot of gold, you couldn't take the gold away from him because it would belong to him? That wouldn't be nice to take something away from someone that it belonged to."

Mollie looked at her for a moment and then replied,

17

"But he would be knowin' where he could be findin' another pot o' gold. That he would."

"But suppose he had to work many long years and save to fill that pot with gold, like you had to work for your food when you lived in Ireland?" Celia asked.

Mollie didn't reply to that but asked another question. "Where be that Indian uncle? He helped me look for leprechauns in Ireland, that he did."

"Uncle Ned," Mandie said. "He's not actually my uncle. He was my father's Cherokee friend. He and his family will probably meet up with us on the mountain at sunrise Sunday."

"On the mountain? Sunrise?" Mollie asked.

"Yes, we will be going up the mountain Sunday to see the sun rise and to hear the Easter sermon," Mandie explained.

"Then kin we look for leprechauns on the mountain?" Mollie asked, looking at Mandie and then at Celia.

"There aren't any leprechauns on the mountain," Mandie told her. "We'll find something else to do up there. We'll sing."

"Sing? And kin we dance, too?" Mollie asked.

Mandie was becoming impatient with the young girl. "No, Mollie, we will not dance," she said. "Easter is a special holy day. We'll be celebrating the time that Jesus rose from His tomb."

"Celebratin'? Will we be havin' a party?" Mollie asked. "Like a birthday party?"

Mandie got to her feet and said to Celia, "Let's take this child to Aunt Lou and ask her to explain a few things. I don't seem to be getting anywhere with it myself."

Celia smiled and also rose. "You are doing better than I have been able to do. But Aunt Lou sounds like the perfect teacher."

Mandie reached for Mollie's hand as she still sat on the floor. "Come on, Mollie, we want you to meet Aunt Lou. You'll love her, I'm sure. She's in charge of everything here—cooking the food, sewing clothes, and running everything."

Mollie stood up without saying a word and allowed Mandie and Celia to take her down the hallway to the kitchen. When Mandie pushed open the door, she found not only Aunt Lou but Liza, Jenny the cook, and her husband, Abraham, all working toward getting the evening meal ready. They stopped what they were doing to stare at Mollie.

"Here's dat lil' angel from Ireland," Aunt Lou said with a big smile.

Mollie frowned at her and said, "I don't be no angel. Mollie I be."

Aunt Lou quickly walked toward her, holding out her arms. "I knows you ain't no real angel," she said as she bent down. "Come to Aunt Lou."

Mollie allowed the woman to embrace her as she asked, "Will ye be me aunt? Celia and her mither they look and look for me aunt and don't find her. Will ye be me aunt?" She looked up into Aunt Lou's smiling face.

" 'Course I'll be yo' aunt," Aunt Lou said as she squeezed the little girl tightly. "Now you jes' call me Aunt Lou and I'll be proud to be yo' aunt."

Mollie, still staring at the woman, asked, "Do ye be

needin' a pot o' gold then?''

Aunt Lou glanced at Mandie with a puzzled look and replied, ''A pot of gold? Whut would I do wid a pot of gold? I don't need no gold.''

Mollie looked up at Mandie and said, ''Then I don't be havin' to take his pot o' gold when I find a leprechaun.''

Aunt Lou straightened up and looked at Mandie. Mollie held on to Aunt Lou's big white apron.

''Oh, Aunt Lou, it's all so confusing,'' Mandie told her. ''Mollie needs a teacher, and I think you'd be better at that than I am. She just doesn't understand anything that I try to explain. Please say you'll help.''

''Liza done told me whut was said in de parlor a while ago,'' the old woman replied. ''I'll see whut I kin do. Aftuh while, dat is. Right now we'se got to git supper done.'' She patted Mollie on the top of her head and said to her, ''Now I'll be yo' aunt, but you's got to go back to de parlor so I kin git dis heah food cooked, you heah?''

Mollie looked up at the woman and asked as she pulled on her apron, ''If I be goin' back to the parlor, ye won't go 'way some place, will ye? Will ye, I say?''

''No, no, I won't be goin' no place,'' Aunt Lou promised as she pulled her apron out of Mollie's hand. ''I

20

stays right heah in dis kitchen till I gits de supper on de table so you kin eat. Ain't you hungry now?'' She moved toward the stove.

"I may be a little hungry," Mollie agreed. "What do ye be wantin' me to do to pay fer it?" She still looked at the woman.

"I be wantin' you to go back to de parlor now," Aunt Lou told her.

"Aunt Lou, she hasn't met everyone else," Mandie said, and taking Mollie by the hand she led her over to Jenny and Abraham, who had been listening to the conversation. "Mollie, this is Jenny and her husband, Abraham. And you already know Liza over there."

Mollie stopped to look Jenny and Abraham over.

"Howdy, little missy," Abraham said with a big grin.

"And you come all de way 'cross dat big ocean from Ireland," Jenny said.

"No, I come from Virginny with Celia and her mither," Mollie informed her. "Before that I be in Ireland."

"Ireland, where dey has leprechauns," Abraham said, still grinning.

Mandie took a quick breath and said, "Abraham, please don't mention the word."

"Leprechauns, ye say," Mollie replied, her blue eyes opening wide. Then she leaned toward the old man and whispered, "Do ye be havin' leprechauns here, I say?"

Mandie rolled her eyes at Abraham and shook her head behind Mollie's back.

Abraham quickly said to Mollie, "Ain't no sech thing as leprechauns in dis heah place. Only find dem in Ireland."

"Oh no," Mandie groaned under her breath.

"Will ye go to Ireland with me and hunt for leprechauns then?" Mollie whispered as she moved closer to the man.

"One o' dese days we'll jes' do dat. Right now I has to git de wood fo' de stove," Abraham said as he looked at Mandie, quickly walked toward the back door, and went outside.

"One day soon we be goin' to Ireland then," Mollie called to him.

Snowball, who had been sleeping under the cook-stove, stood up, stretched, yawned, and ran toward Mollie. The little girl quickly picked him up.

"Come on, Mollie, we have to go back to the parlor so all these people can get supper done," Mandie told her.

Mollie held on to Snowball and followed Mandie and Celia out the door. The three walked down the hallway toward the parlor.

"I can see that we're going to have some interesting hoLidays," Celia remarked.

"I'm hoping Aunt Lou can make her understand what the holidays are all about," Mandie said with a big sigh.

Part Two

After supper was over that night, Mollie insisted on going to the kitchen to visit with Aunt Lou, whom she now claimed for her own aunt.

When everyone rose from the table in the dining room, Elizabeth asked, "Would anyone be interested in a short walk? I feel the need to stretch my legs."

"Certainly," Jane Hamilton agreed. "Count me in."

"And of course I will go along with you ladies," John Shaw said, smiling at his wife, Elizabeth. Turning to the girls, he asked, "Are y'all coming along?"

"I be goin' to see me aunt Lou," Mollie quickly insisted. She hurried to Aunt Lou, who came into the dining room at that moment. The little girl grabbed the woman's big white apron to get her attention. "Kin I come to see ye now? Kin I, I say?"

The big woman looked down at her and said, "Soon

as we finish wid de supper work. Den we sit down in de kitchen and talk, you and me.''

"Mollie, come with us until Aunt Lou is finished," Jane Hamilton called across the room. The adults were going into the hallway.

"I will help me aunt so we kin hurry," Mollie told her, still holding on to the corner of Aunt Lou's apron as the woman moved about the room.

"No, Mollie, we want you to come with us," Mandie told her. She stepped across the room toward her.

Mollie tried to hide behind Aunt Lou as she said, "I be wantin' to talk to me aunt, that I do."

"Leave huh be, my chile," the woman said to Mandie with a big smile. "I'll take huh to de kitchen wid me whilst y'all gone."

"Well, all right, Aunt Lou," Mandie said. "Please be sure she doesn't run off somewhere." She went back across the room to join Celia.

"Don't worry now. I'll keep huh right under my sight," the old woman replied.

As Mandie and Celia went out into the hallway to catch up with the adults, Mandie heard Mollie say, "They don't be wantin' to look for leprechauns."

"Now dat's something we'se got to talk about," Mandie heard Aunt Lou reply.

"I sure hope Aunt Lou can make Mollie understand that we don't have leprechauns," Mandie said with a deep sigh.

"So do I. She has been about to drive us all crazy back home with this talk about leprechauns," Celia agreed.

The two girls quickly got their wraps from the hall

tree and followed the adults out into the chilly evening air.

Jason Bond, John Shaw's caretaker, was turning into the driveway on his horse as they walked toward the road. John Shaw hurried to meet him, and Mr. Bond stepped down from his horse. They stood and talked.

"Well, I just now realized Mr. Jason was not at the supper table with us," Mandie said. "With Mollie entertaining everyone, I didn't miss him."

Elizabeth and Jane had walked on ahead, and the girls hurried to catch up with them. Mandie glanced at her uncle and Mr. Bond as she passed near them. They were deep in a conversation, but she couldn't hear what they were saying. "I wonder what they are talking about. They act as though it's confidential," she said to her friend.

Celia looked at the men and said to Mandie, "Probably some business matter or other."

"But I'd like to know what about," Mandie replied, grinning at her friend.

"Oh, Mandie, you're always trying to keep up with every little thing that's going on," Celia said with a laugh.

"But it might be something interesting," Mandie said, looking at her with a big smile as they walked.

John Shaw quickly caught up with the girls on his way to join Elizabeth and Jane. "Come on, you two slowpokes," he said, laughing as he went ahead.

"Race you to the corner!" Mandie yelled at him. She picked up her long skirts and rushed toward the gate, where Elizabeth and Jane had stopped to wait. "Come on, Celia!" she called back to her friend.

Celia quickly followed and John Shaw broke into a run behind Mandie. Jane and Elizabeth watched in surprise.

Since Mandie had a head start and the corner was not far away, she got there first and Celia was close behind her. As John Shaw caught up, Mandie laughed and asked, "Now who is the slowpoke?"

"You didn't give me a fair chance. I was not expecting that," John Shaw said, pretending to fuss.

Mandie straightened her long skirts and grinned at him. "You should always be prepared. That's what they are teaching us at school," she said.

John Shaw looked down at her and replied, "I'll remember that."

Elizabeth and Jane had hurried to catch up with them, and Elizabeth asked, "What's wrong?"

"You had us worried for a minute," Jane Hamilton said.

"Uncle John called us slowpokes, and we just wanted to prove to him that we're not," Mandie said with a big grin.

"Well, please don't do that again," Elizabeth said as she and Jane walked on.

"That was too much excitement," Jane added.

John Shaw started to catch up with the two women and Mandie touched his hand to stop him. "Mr. Jason didn't have supper with us," she said, hoping her uncle would volunteer some information.

"No, because I sent him on an errand. Now I must catch up with the ladies," John Shaw said, grinning down at her and hurrying on.

"Oh, shucks!" Mandie said. "An errand? Must have

been an awfully important errand for Mr. Jason to miss supper.'' She still stood there.

"Come on, Mandie, let's walk," Celia urged her.

Mandie looked back toward the house. "Maybe Mr. Jason would tell me where he's been," she said as she slowly followed Celia.

"Mandie, don't count on it," Celia said. "It's probably some of your uncle's business matters that don't concern anyone else."

"I'd still like to know where he went," Mandie said.

The girls followed the adults to the square downtown. They strolled around the courthouse yard, Elizabeth and John greeting friends here and there who were also out for exercise. Shortly thereafter they all returned to the house.

Mandie looked in the parlor for Mr. Bond, then in the dining room and the kitchen, but he was nowhere to be found. However, Mollie was in the kitchen. She was sitting in Aunt Lou's lap as the old woman was evidently reading the Bible to her when Mandie and Celia opened the door. Snowball was asleep at Aunt Lou's feet.

Mollie sat up straight when she saw the girls and said, "Me aunt is readin' a good book to me. It be all about these people called angels. They be like leprechauns. Not everybody kin see them." She seemed interested.

Aunt Lou shook her head where Mollie couldn't see her and gave Mandie a disappointed look as she closed the Bible.

Mandie nodded back and then said to Mollie, "Let's go in the parlor where everyone is and let Aunt Lou get some rest now."

Mollie quickly slid down to stand up, barely missing Snowball, who immediately rose and moved out of her way.

As Mandie and Celia walked toward the parlor, Mollie kept up a steady stream of talk about what Aunt Lou had told her. Snowball followed.

"The angel people are all white, me aunt thinks," Mollie said, looking up at Mandie. "And sometime they do good things, but there be one bad one that God didn't like, and He threw him all the way down to where the Devil be. And he can't iver come back to live with the good angel people because he's been bad. But me aunt Lou thinks God won't throw us down there for being bad if we be sorry. So when I be bad, all I have to do is be sorry, and I always do be sorry when I be bad. Do ye be sorry when ye be bad, Mandie? Do ye?" She tugged on Mandie's hand.

Mandie smiled down at the little girl and said, "Yes, I'm always sorry for being bad, but I try real hard not to be bad. And I always ask God to forgive me."

"Me aunt Lou said she would show me how to talk to God tomorrow when she reads me more of that book, because I don't be knowin' how to ask God to forgive me when I've been bad, and I need to know real soon just in case I be bad agin," Mollie said.

"Oh, Mollie, I'm sure Aunt Lou will be able to teach you about God," Celia said.

They came to the doorway of the parlor. The adults were already there, but Mandie noticed Jason Bond was not with them. He seemed to have completely disappeared after they saw him in the driveway. Mandie and Celia sat down at the far end of the room away from the adults, and Mandie watched to see what Mollie would do or say. The little girl frowned as she stared at Elizabeth and then at John while she stood in the middle of the floor. Then she quickly ran to join the girls on the settee, scrambling up between them. Snowball sat down at Mandie's feet and looked at Mollie.

Suddenly Mollie turned to Mandie and asked, "Do ye be thinkin' Snowball might be a angel cat? He do be white."

Mandie and Celia both smiled at her as Mandie said, "No, Mollie, he's just a real live white cat."

"Why don't we take Mollie around the house and show her all the rooms and everything? By that time it will be bedtime," Celia suggested under her breath.

Mandie stood up and said, "That's a good idea. Only we won't go in the secret tunnel. That would be s-c-a-r-y at night, I think." She spelled out the word but Mollie had heard the words "secret tunnel."

"Do ye be havin' a secret tunnel in this house, do ye, Mandie?" Mollie asked as she and Celia also rose.

"Well, that's a long story, and it will have to wait until tomorrow," Mandie told her.

"But tomorrow be a long way off, Mandie," Mollie protested. "Tell me now, please, I say."

"Mollie, we don't have time right now for that," Mandie told her firmly. "Come on. We'll show you the rest of the house."

"Then tomorrow ye will tell me about the secret tunnel, be ye not forgittin' that," Mollie said.

"If I forget, you just remind me tomorrow," Mandie said with a sigh of exasperation as she looked at Celia.

Celia leaned forward to whisper in Mandie's ear.

"This isn't the worst. Just you wait until we put her to bed," she said.

"Oh no!" Mandie exclaimed.

————

And when bedtime came, Mollie insisted on sleeping in a room by herself. The girls were in Mandie's room later that night.

"Don't you want to sleep in here with me, Mollie?" Mandie asked as the three got ready for bed.

"No, that I not be wantin' to do," Mollie replied as she pulled her nightgown over her head. "I be wantin' a big bed all by meself like I be havin' at Celia's house."

"You could sleep with me in the next room," Celia suggested, pushing open the door to the adjoining bedroom.

Mollie looked through the doorway and started into the room. "I will be sleepin' in this big bed by meself," she said as she walked over to the bed in that room and climbed up on top of it.

"Well, if you insist, wait until I turn down the covers," Mandie said. She hurried to remove the counterpane as Mollie slid back down to the floor. She quickly threw back the quilt and sheet and said, "All right, Mollie, it's all ready for you. Please don't fall out during the night."

Mollie climbed back up on the bed and scooted down beneath the covers as Mandie turned them back up. "Good night, Mandie, and ye, too, Celia," the little girl said as she curled up and closed her eyes.

"Good night, Mollie, I hope you have a good night's

33

sleep," Mandie said, starting back toward her own room.

"Good night, Mollie. If you change your mind about sleeping alone, you can come and get in the bed with Mandie and me," Celia told her.

Mollie muttered, "Mmmm."

Mandie left the door between the rooms slightly open, and she and Celia got in her bed. Snowball curled up at their feet.

"Uncle John must have sent Mr. Jason off somewhere again. I never did see him after he got back this afternoon," Mandie remarked.

"Yes, or maybe he was tired and just went on to his room for the night," Celia replied.

"Maybe if I get up real early I can catch him, and maybe, just maybe, he will tell me what the errand was that Uncle John sent him on," Mandie said, snuggling down under the covers. "I know he's always the first one up in the mornings, so I'll hurry and go to sleep so I will wake up early. If you wake up first, Celia, will you please wake me?"

"All right. Good night, Mandie," Celia agreed as she turned over on her side of the bed and then added, "Mollie will probably wake us both up. She gets up before daylight sometimes."

"Then I hope she does in the morning," Mandie said as she tried to relax and go to sleep.

The girls drifted off to sleep. Later Mandie was suddenly awakened by a heavy weight dropping on top of her feet. She quickly sat up, and in the dim light from the window, she saw that it was Snowball who had evidently been off the bed and had returned with a jump

on the covers. She moved her feet out from under him as he circled around.

"Snowball, please lie down and be still," she whispered to the cat. She glanced through the open doorway to the other bedroom and said to herself, "I might as well see if Mollie is all right since I'm awake."

Mandie threw back the covers on her side of the bed, careful not to wake Celia, and she slid off the high bed to her feet. Going over to the doorway, she squinted her eyes to look into the darkness of the other bedroom. The draperies were open, allowing the moonlight to stream across the room, clearly showing that Mollie was not in the bed.

"Mollie!" Mandie called softly as she stepped inside the room and looked around. There was no one there. She walked over to the mantelpiece to look at the clock in the dim light. "Three o'clock!" she exclaimed. "Where is Mollie? It's too early to get up."

Mandie went to the open hall door and looked up and down the hallway. There was no sign of the girl. She would have to get her shoes and robe before going farther.

Celia was still asleep when Mandie reached for her robe on a chair in her room, but as she bent to put on her shoes, she accidentally dropped one and the small thud it made on the carpet woke Celia.

"Mandie, is it time to get up?" Celia asked, sitting up in bed and rubbing her eyes.

"No, Celia, it's only three o'clock, but Mollie is not in her bed and I'll have to go find her," Mandie said with an exasperated sigh as she got her shoes on.

Celia quickly jumped out of bed, grabbed her robe

and shoes, and said, "I'll help you find her. She is bad about doing this."

"Where does she go? What does she do when she gets up so early?" Mandie asked as she started toward the door and Celia followed. Snowball silently trailed along behind them.

"All kinds of things," Celia replied as they stepped into the long hallway that was dimly lighted by a lamp sitting on a table near the stairway. "Sometimes we find her eating food out of the icebox, and sometimes she's curled up asleep in the parlor. We never know where to look for her."

"Oh goodness!" Mandie exclaimed as they hurried toward the staircase. "Does she ever go outdoors?"

"Not that we know of," Celia replied as they rushed down the stairwell.

Mandie picked up a lighted lamp at the foot of the stairs, and the two girls hastily searched the whole downstairs. Mollie was nowhere to be found. All the outside doors were securely locked for the night.

"Unless she went up to the third floor, she must have gone outside, but I can't imagine how she got outside with all the doors locked," Mandie said as they stopped in the hallway at the foot of the steps.

"Or she could have gone down in the cellar or up in the attic. You know she's not afraid of anything," Celia said.

"In the cellar?" Mandie questioned. "Come on. Let's go look. The door to the cellar is kept locked."

Mandie led the way to the cellar door in the back hallway next to the kitchen. She hurried to hold the lamp up so she could see the latch on the door. "She

37

can't be in the cellar. See? The latch is on, so she couldn't go inside the cellar and lock the door out here behind her."

"Well, I'm glad we don't have to go down there," Celia remarked as she looked at the locked door.

Suddenly there was a metallic sound at the outside back door that was near where the girls stood. They both heard it and silently stood waiting and listening. Snowball's ears pricked up as he ran toward the door.

"Somebody is coming in," Celia whispered as she moved closer to Mandie.

"Whoever it is has a key," Mandie whispered back as she watched the door.

The door opened quickly and Mr. Jason Bond stepped inside. He stopped in surprise when he saw the girls.

Mandie let out a breath of relief as she said, "Thank goodness that was you, Mr. Jason!"

"What are you two doing down here this time of night?" Mr. Bond asked as he closed the door behind him. Snowball rubbed around his legs.

"We're looking for Mollie. She's not in her bedroom," Mandie explained. "Where have you been this time of night, Mr. Jason?"

"On an errand for your uncle," Mr. Bond said, coming down the hallway toward them. "Now, we probably ought to find that little girl. I'll help y'all look for her." He removed his coat and hat and hung them on the hall tree.

"We've already searched this floor and she's not here," Mandie told him. "And she can't be in the cellar

38

because the door is locked. And all the outside doors are locked."

"Then I suppose we ought to look upstairs," Mr. Bond told the girls. "But we're going to have to be awfully quiet so we won't wake everybody up." He picked up the lamp burning on the table nearby.

Mr. Bond led the way up the stairs to the second floor, and at the top of the steps he turned and motioned for the girls to be quiet. Snowball padded along with him. Even though Celia and her mother and Mollie were visiting, there were several unoccupied bedrooms, and Mr. Bond opened the door to each one as he came to them, stepped inside with the lighted lamp, and the girls quickly followed.

"We should look everywhere in everything," Celia whispered to them. "Mollie has a way of hiding in strange places, even under beds and in wardrobes."

Mandie stooped down to look under the huge bed that was high enough off the floor for someone to scoot under it. "Not there," she muttered as she backed off and stood up.

Celia had gone to the wardrobe and was opening the huge doors on it while Mr. Bond searched behind some of the massive pieces of furniture in the room. Mandie watched and then led the way out into the hallway and into the next unoccupied room. Finally they came to the last room and still had not found Mollie. And they did not find her in any of the unoccupied rooms on the third floor either.

"I suppose we ought to go up to the attic next," Mr. Bond said in a low voice to the girls as they stood at the end of the hallway.

"I suppose so," Mandie said with a sigh. "Mollie has to be in the house somewhere."

"And it'll soon be time for everyone to get up," Celia said. Looking at Mandie, she added, "You wanted to get up early, remember?"

Mandie suddenly realized what her friend was talking about. She had wanted to catch Mr. Bond and ask him about his errand, but here he was and he had practically ignored her question when he first came in the back door. How was she going to find out exactly where he had been? There must be some mystery attached to Mr. Bond's goings and comings because he and her uncle didn't seem to want to talk about whatever they were doing.

Mr. Bond started down the hallway toward the steps to the attic. He stopped and looked back at the girls. "Now, if y'all don't want to go up to the attic with me, I can look around up there by myself." He paused and grinned at them as he added, "I'm not afraid."

Both the girls laughed softly.

"I'm not afraid of the dark old attic," Mandie said in a low voice. "Let's go."

"And neither am I," Celia added.

The three slowly and carefully ascended the stairs to the attic. Mandie knew some of the steps creaked, and she tried to avoid them. She certainly didn't want her mother or Uncle John or Celia's mother to wake and come to see what was going on.

Mandie was still carrying the lamp she had picked up at the foot of the main staircase, and Mr. Bond had the one he had brought from the downstairs hallway. Together the lamps illuminated the huge dark attic enough for them to walk around between the many, many boxes, trunks, pieces of furniture, and other items in the room.

"Mollie," Mandie softly called as she went to one side and Mr. Bond investigated the other part. Celia stayed close to Mandie. Snowball had followed them, and he playfully pounced about.

Mr. Bond stepped over to Mandie's side to say, "Don't forget. Liza and Aunt Lou have rooms beneath here."

"Right," Mandie agreed in a whisper. She continued on around the room.

After a while Mr. Bond motioned to the two girls to follow him as he went toward the door. Mandie and Celia caught up with him, and he said in a low whisper, "That little girl is not here. Let's go back down to the first floor. And please be quiet."

"Yes, sir," the two girls spoke in unison as they followed him out of the attic, down the stairway, all the way to the first floor. He stopped at the bottom of the staircase. Snowball ran on down the hallway toward the front of the house.

"I am going to the kitchen to find a bite to eat since I missed supper last night," Mr. Bond told them. "I don't know what to say about the little girl. She's just not in this house. Maybe she'll come back on her own. I'll look around after I eat." He went toward the back hallway.

"We'll go to the parlor and wait for you, Mr. Bond," Mandie told him.

Mandie and Celia sat down on a settee in the parlor after Mandie had placed the lighted lamp on a table. The fire in the fireplace the night before had turned to cold ashes and the room was chilly. The girls curled up in their long heavy robes and discussed the situation. Snowball was already there sitting on the hearth.

"This is unbelievable," Celia remarked. "How could Mollie disappear with all the doors locked?"

Mandie suddenly had an idea. "Oh, Celia, I know of one possibility," she said quickly. "Maybe Mollie went to somebody's room and got in the bed with them— your mother, or even Aunt Lou. Maybe she got scared all by herself in that room we put her in."

"I don't believe she's ever done that before, but then this is a strange house to her," Celia replied. "But, Mandie, we certainly can't go looking in people's rooms while they're asleep."

"No, I guess not," Mandie agreed. "But this has me really puzzled."

"I think we should go back to bed. We've done the best we can to find her, and we do need a little more sleep before breakfast time," Celia said.

Mandie yawned in spite of herself. "I know, but I was hoping Mr. Jason would come in here before he goes to bed," she said. "And maybe he'll tell us where he's been."

"Mandie, I don't think he's going to tell us a single thing," Celia said. "He didn't explain anything when he told us he had been on an errand. Why don't we just go back to bed?"

"You go ahead. I'll go after Mr. Jason comes back in here," Mandie told her friend.

Snowball suddenly jumped up from his place on the hearth and meowed loudly. He raced across the room

and jumped up on a table by a window that was on the front of the house.

Mandie quickly stood up and said, "Snowball, get down from there!" She ran over to the table as she called to Celia. "Look! Look!"

Celia hurried after her.

"There's Mollie!" Mandie exclaimed as she saw the little girl outside on the porch trying to raise the window. "And she must have gone out through this window!" She reached up and locked it as Mollie watched. "I'll let her in through the front door." She motioned for Mollie to go on down the porch.

When Mandie opened the front door, Mollie was standing there in her nightgown and was terribly excited about something. "Come to the parlor," Mandie told her as she went back down the hallway. Mollie followed.

"Mollie, where have you been?" Celia asked as she met them in the doorway to the parlor.

"I be seein' one of them angel people like me aunt Lou told me about," Mollie said, rushing excitedly about the room. "Me aunt Lou was right. They do be angel people, all white like she be sayin'. The angel people kin talk, too. But the angel people flew away while I be watchin'. All white and—"

"Mollie, come here and sit down," Mandie told her as she grasped the little girl's hand and led her to the settee, where the three of them sat down. Snowball meowed loudly and jumped up between Mollie and Celia.

"But, Mandie, I be sayin'—"

"Mollie!" Mandie said loudly. "Please be quiet a minute. I want to ask you some questions." She still held the little girl's hand.

Mollie jerked her hand out of Mandie's and said, "I be quiet if'n ye don't be squeezin' me hand." She flexed her fingers, pretending to be hurt.

Mandie quickly reached down and kissed the little girl's hand. "I'm sorry, Mollie, I didn't mean to hurt you," she said. "Now let's begin at the beginning. Where have you been? We've looked the house over for you, and it's the middle of night. We all need to be in bed and asleep."

Mollie looked up at her with her bright blue eyes and said, "But, Mandie, I was in the bed, and this angel people—I really be sure it was a leprechaun angel, that it was—it came to me bed and asked me to follow it. So I—"

"You must have been dreaming, Mollie," Celia said. "The house was all locked up and nobody could get in."

Mollie looked at Celia and said, "Oh, but mistaken ye be. All the doors was locked, but this leprechaun angel showed me the way to the window over there. It was open, it was. And it says to me real softlike, 'follow, follow,' and I follow. I be thinkin' this leprechaun angel may be takin' me to its pot o' gold, so I go out the window—"

"Where did you go when you went out the window, Mollie?" Celia asked.

"There be a house back there with horses in it, there is," Mollie told her. "I be followin' this leprechaun angel, and it went into this house, and I followed just like it told me, but then I couldn't find it, I couldn't. It went plumb away, bless Pat, plumb away, gone." She shook her head sadly.

"You were gone a long time, Mollie, because we

have been searching the whole house for you," Mandie told her.

"I be gone a long time because I be lookin' to find the leprechaun angel, but that I could not do," Mollie explained. "I looked and looked and looked, in all the bushes and behind all the trees, but it went away, it did."

"What did this thing, or person, look like? Was it tall or short? A man or a woman? Did it say anything else to you?" Mandie asked as she studied the little girl's face.

"It was tall—taller than you, Mandie," Mollie explained. "But I don't be knowin' what it might be lookin' like 'cause it didn't have a face. It was covered up all over with white linen, just like me mither made in Belfast Mill, and it said nary a word to me but 'follow, follow,' and so I followed. But it floated away, sure it did, and I looked and looked and could not find it. Why do ye be supposin' it told me to follow it and then it would not let me find it agin?" She looked at Mandie and then at Celia with a puzzled expression on her face.

Mandie and Celia looked at each other over her head, neither one knowing what to make of this tale.

At that moment Jason Bond came into the parlor. He smiled when he saw Mollie. "So you found her, did you?" he said to Mandie and Celia. He sat down in a chair.

"No, not exactly," Mandie replied, and she explained what had taken place. "So now we don't know exactly what happened."

"At least she's back, safe and sound," Mr. Bond said. Lowering his voice he added, "You might try turning the key, you know, tonight." He made a motion to indicate locking the door.

"If I can figure out how to do that without a loud protest," Mandie replied. She noticed that Mollie was listening to every word, but she doubted that the little girl would understand what they were saying.

Jason Bond stood up and said, "I believe it's time for me to get a little sleep. Gotta get up early again in the morning." He started toward the doorway.

"Mr. Jason, do you have to go on another errand for my uncle?" Mandie asked quickly.

Mr. Bond stopped to look back at her and to say, "Now, you know your uncle's business is confidential and I can't discuss it with anyone, so I think you shouldn't worry your pretty little head over such things. And I also think you girls, all three of you, should crawl back in your beds and get some sleep. Otherwise y'all are going to be awfully sleepyheaded tomorrow. Night, night, now." He went out into the hallway.

"Guess we might as well," Mandie said as she rose from the settee. "Come on, Mollie, we're all going back to bed."

"Are ye sure we must go to bed?" Mollie asked, standing up.

Mandie smiled down at her and said, "Yes, I am sure."

"And this time, Mollie, you must stay in your bed for the rest of the night," Celia told her.

"But what if the leprechaun angel comes back to see me and wants me to go with it?" Mollie asked.

"Mollie, there is no such thing as a leprechaun angel," Mandie told her.

47

"But, Mandie, I just told ye I saw one," Mollie argued. She followed Mandie toward the door.

"We'll talk about that tomorrow," Mandie told her. "Right now we are all going to bed, and we are going to stay in our beds until it's time to get up for breakfast."

The three girls went out into the hallway and up the stairs to their rooms. Mandie and Celia both stayed in the room with Mollie until she was tucked in bed.

"Now, we will be sleeping in my room," Mandie told her, "and we will be looking in the door here once in a while during the night to see that you are still in bed, so please don't get up and roam around again. Do you understand?"

Mollie looked up at Mandie with her bright blue eyes, pushed back her carrot-red hair, and with a frown she replied, "I be here, Mandie. I promise, I say."

"All right then, good night," Mandie said, stooping over to plant a kiss on the little girl's forehead.

To Mandie's surprise, Mollie quickly wiped the kiss away with her hand. Then she scooted down deeper into the covers, turned over, and closed her eyes.

Mandie straightened up and looked at Celia. Celia smiled at her and said, "That's normal."

Mandie closed the door to the hallway, turned the key, and took the key with her into her room, where she dropped it into a tall vase.

As Celia got back into bed, Mandie said, "I'll be right back. I just want to look one more time to be sure that window is locked downstairs."

"I'm sure it is because we locked it," Celia answered as she pulled the cover up.

Mandie hurried down the stairs and into the parlor

and over to the window. The hallway was lighted by a lamp sitting on a table there, but the parlor was dark enough that Mandie could see the moonlight outside. She gave the lock a quick twist, but it was still locked. Then just as she turned to go back upstairs she thought she saw something move outside on the porch. She quickly leaned against the glass to see what it was.

"I know I saw something," she muttered to herself, peering out.

Suddenly a white form seemed to float off the porch and around the house. Mandie rubbed her eyes and looked again.

"I must be imagining things after all the excitement tonight," she muttered to herself.

Mandie stood there watching for a few minutes, but there was no sign of anything outside. Finally deciding nothing was there, she left the parlor and went back up to her room.

When she crawled back into bed, Mandie saw that Celia was already asleep. But she lay awake for a long time thinking about the possibility of something white on the front porch in the dark.

"I'm getting as bad as Mollie with my imagination," she silently told herself. "And I've got to go to sleep. If it was really something, it would be already gone by now anyway. Tomorrow I'll look around just in case there is something disturbed on the porch."

She finally dropped off to sleep and dreamed of white forms floating all around her, everywhere she looked.

Part Three

The next day, much to Mandie's relief, Mollie had evidently forgotten about the secret tunnel that she had promised to show the little girl. And the next few days Mollie stayed close to Aunt Lou and insisted on her reading more from the "good book" about the angel people. Mandie and Celia checked on Mollie now and then to be sure she was not bothering Aunt Lou too much as she followed the old woman about the house. Then on Friday, Mandie was up early and found Mollie in the kitchen sitting on Aunt Lou's lap by the cook-stove.

"Oh, Mandie," Mollie said as she quickly looked across the room at Mandie. "Ye don't be havin' leprechauns, but ye do be havin' these angel people. Me aunt Lou knows all about them, she does."

Mandie, standing in the doorway with Celia, smiled

at her and said, "Now, Mollie, you have to let Aunt Lou rest now and then. She has lots of other things to do."

Before Mollie could reply, Aunt Lou smiled and said, "Now, my chile, I can handle this lil' girl all right. She's jes' starved for attention, and she's a-learnin' real fast."

"I told Aunt Lou about the leprechaun angel that came to see me that night, and Aunt Lou said for me to come and git her to see the leprechaun angel, if'n it comes back to see me, she did," Mollie said to Mandie. "She be wantin' to see it, too, she does."

"But, remember, Mollie," Mandie told her, "if you do see anything at all anymore, you are not to get out of bed and go chasing after it. You must come and let me know first."

"That's right, Mollie. You are not allowed to run around the house after everyone has gone to sleep," Celia added.

"And guess who is coming in on the train this morning?" Mandie said, smiling at the little girl.

Mollie frowned for a moment and then she said, "Makes no nevermind. I've got me aunt Lou to talk to now. I don't be needin' nobody else."

"Not even Grandmother?" Mandie asked teasingly.

"Me grandmither is coming on the train?" Mollie asked and then quickly added, "But I be busy with me aunt Lou, reading the good book about the angel people."

"Also, Uncle Ned will be here this morning, and he's bringing his wife, Morning Star, and his granddaughter, Sallie," Mandie continued with a big grin.

Mollie quickly shook her head and said, "I don't be needin' that uncle named Ned to help me find a leprechaun because now I want to find one of these angel people."

"And my friend Joe Woodard and his parents will arrive in time for church services today," Mandie continued.

"I don't be knowin' this Joe friend, Mandie, so I'll jes' stay in here with me aunt Lou," Mollie told her.

Mandie sighed and said to Aunt Lou, "I leave her for you to handle."

"Don't you be worryin' none 'bout it, my chile. I take care of ev'rything," Aunt Lou said, smiling and smoothing Mollie's carrot-red hair. "You and yo' friend there jes' go on in de dinin' room and eat yo' breakfus'. Liza in there awaitin' fo' ev'rybody. Dis heah lil' miss dun eat wid me."

Everyone came down to breakfast early that morning, and before the meal was finished Dr. and Mrs. Woodard and Joe were knocking on the front door, followed in a little while by Uncle Ned, his wife, Morning Star, and granddaughter, Sallie. Then, the train came in early and Mrs. Taft, Mandie's grandmother, was brought from the depot by a friend of the Shaws who was meeting someone else at the depot. Jason Bond had just hitched up the carriage, and all the young people were waiting in the front hallway to ride to the station to meet the train. They kept watching out the front window for Mr. Bond to bring the carriage around.

Suddenly Mollie jumped down from the chair where she was sitting in order to see outside. "Mandie! Mandie! There be me grandmither!" she yelled excitedly as she raced for the front door.

Mandie instantly followed her and pulled the big

door open. Sure enough, there was Mrs. Taft coming up the walkway. Mollie pushed her way around Mandie and raced outside to meet her. Mandie followed.

"Grandmither! Grandmither!" Mollie exclaimed as she stopped in front of the lady.

Mrs. Taft smiled and bent down to take Mollie's hand. She looked at Mandie and said, "It seems I have two granddaughters now."

Mandie quickly reached to squeeze the lady's other hand. "Oh, Grandmother, how did you get here so early? We were going to meet the train."

Mr. Bond came down the driveway in the carriage and stopped when he saw Mrs. Taft. "Good morning, ma'am," he called to her. "Where is your luggage?"

"The Bennetts dropped me off, and I left the trunk at the station if you would please get it for me," Mrs. Taft called back to him. "Thank you."

"My pleasure, ma'am," Mr. Bond replied as he started to drive out of the yard. But suddenly he was overtaken by all the other young people who had been listening and who were determined to get a ride to the depot and back. Joe, Celia, and Sallie all piled into the vehicle.

"Come on, Mandie!" Joe called to her. "You, too, Mollie!" he added.

"I'll wait here. I want to talk to my grandmother," Mandie replied.

"And I do not want to go, I don't," Mollie said, clasping her other hand over the hand Mrs. Taft was holding.

Mandie's friends waved good-bye as Mr. Bond drove off.

"Grandmother, I'm so glad you are here and that

you are able to see Mollie again," Mandie said as they walked toward the front door.

"Grandmither," Mollie quickly said. "Mandie does not have leprechauns. She has angel people, all white like Snowball. Me aunt Lou has been reading to me all about them—"

"Mollie, we have to explain to Grandmother. She doesn't know what we are talking about," Mandie interrupted her.

"Whatever you are talking about, please let me get inside and get comfortable before we get into an explanation," Mrs. Taft said with a smile for both girls.

Mollie didn't say anything else, but as soon as Mrs. Taft spoke to the other adults in the parlor and told them she was going up to her room, Mollie followed her up the steps and Mandie came after her.

"Mollie, let's let Grandmother rest a little while before we talk to her," she told the little girl as they stopped on the staircase.

"Just bring her on up to my room, dear," Mrs. Taft said as she continued on her way. "I'm anxious to hear what she has to tell me."

Mandie looked up and grinned at Mrs. Taft as she said, "If you say so, Grandmother." And she took Mollie's hand and followed.

After Mrs. Taft had changed into comfortable clothes, she sat down in a big chair by the fire in the fireplace and remarked, "The weather always seems to cool off on Good Friday. The fire feels good." Turning to Mollie, who had not said a word yet, Mrs. Taft asked, "Now tell me all about these angel people you mentioned, dear. Sit right here." She indicated a stool near her.

Mollie frowned as she looked at Mrs. Taft and slowly sat down on the stool without taking her eyes off the lady.

"Well, Mollie, Grandmother wants you to tell her about the angel people you've been talking about. Go ahead and explain," Mandie encouraged her as she sat down nearby.

"Grandmither," Mollie began slowly and then talked as fast as she could. "This angel people, all white and floaty, came to git me to follow it in the night, it did. And I followed it, I did. And it vanished. I couldn't find it anymore." She shook her head sadly.

Mrs. Taft looked at Mandie, and Mandie began explaining what had happened the night Mollie had crawled out of bed and gone outside. She also explained about Aunt Lou trying to teach Mollie about the angels in the Bible.

"Evidently she didn't know anything at all about the Bible until Celia's Aunt Rebecca began teaching her," Mandie said. "And now she has become fast friends with Aunt Lou, who is trying to teach her."

"I certainly hope some progress can be made," Mrs. Taft said thoughtfully, and then turning to Mollie she asked, "Do you know what today is?"

"Today is Friday," Mollie said. "And we are all going to church."

"Do you understand what Easter is all about?" Mrs. Taft asked.

"Oh, Grandmither, those bad people stuck nails in Jesus and hung Him on a cross. Oh, my, it hurt, it did!"

Mollie replied as she shivered all over.

Mrs. Taft looked at her and started to ask another question when Mollie added, "They made Him die, they did. But, no matter, He woke up so He could save us all, He did."

Mrs. Taft smiled at Mollie and said, "You are learning."

———

Later, when everyone attended the church service at noon, Mandie noticed that Mollie, sitting next to her, seemed to be listening to every word the preacher said. But then when the man asked that every head be bowed in prayer, Mandie watched to see that Mollie bowed hers. The little girl saw Mandie looking at her and quickly closed her eyes and bent her head forward. Then Mandie did likewise as she reached to hold Mollie's hand.

While the preacher was praying, Mollie suddenly jerked Mandie's hand and said in a loud whisper, "There's the angel people!" She slid off the pew to her feet.

Mandie quickly grabbed her, pulled her back onto the seat, and put her hand over her mouth. "Shhhhh!" Mandie warned her.

"But, Mandie," Mollie tried to argue in a whisper.

"Shhhhh!" Mandie whispered in Mollie's ear as she put an arm around her.

When the preacher had finished praying, Mandie straightened up to look around and saw everyone in the congregation looking in their direction. Evidently they had all heard the commotion. She could hardly wait to get Mollie out of the church. Uncle Ned was sitting on the other side of Mollie, and he looked at Mandie and shook his head. Mollie caught his glance and immediately moved closer to Mandie.

As soon as the service was over and everyone returned to the house, Mollie immediately disappeared into the kitchen in search of Aunt Lou, and no one discussed Mollie's behavior in church. After dinner, however, Mollie managed to catch Mandie alone in the hallway and the little girl quickly began explaining, "Mandie, that angel people was in the church, it was—"

Mandie stooped down to look straight into Mollie's bright blue eyes and said, "Now, look here, Mollie, you were very disruptive in church today."

"What's disruptive, Mandie?" Mollie asked with a frown.

Mandie sighed and tried to explain, "That was not nice of you to speak out loud like that in church, especially when everyone was supposed to be praying."

"But ye was not prayin', Mandie. Ye was lookin' at me, ye was," Mollie told her.

"You're right, Mollie," Mandie said. "I'm sorry. I should have been praying, too, but I was watching to see if you understood what to do."

"But, Mandie," Mollie said, "that angel people was in the church, I say."

"Mollie, let's you and I make a promise to each other," Mandie said. "Let's not talk about seeing angel people anymore. If you see any, just keep it a secret. Don't let anyone else know, you understand?"

Mollie looked puzzled as she asked, "Kin I tell me aunt Lou about it when I see the angel people? She told me about the angel people in the Bible. Kin I?"

Mandie sighed again as she stood up and said, "All right, you may tell Aunt Lou, but keep it a secret from everyone else. Don't tell anybody else."

"Then I will go see me aunt Lou, that I will," Mollie said as she ran on down the hallway toward the kitchen.

Mandie watched her go and shook her head. How was anyone ever going to teach Mollie anything?

———

On Sunday everyone rose early, dressed in their church clothes, and walked up the mountain to a clearing where the preacher held the sunrise service. Everyone in Franklin—rich, poor, servants and all—made the journey in the early morning dusk. It had rained the night before and a mist hung over their pathway. The wet underbrush dampened their clothes, but no one noticed. They were intent on reaching the peak before the sun showed itself.

Mandie held Mollie's hand as Celia came along the other side. Liza joined them, and she kept watching Mollie. Mollie was a curiosity to her. She had never seen a foreigner before, and she was fascinated with Mollie's speech and actions.

The preacher stood on the uppermost knob of the hill and spoke to the people. Mandie tried to listen and watch Mollie at the same time to be sure she was behaving. At one point Mollie suddenly pulled on her hand and tried to jump up and down, but Mandie gave her a stern look and she quieted down. Then during the singing Mollie tried to get Mandie's attention again, but Mandie squeezed her hand and ignored her. Celia

reached for Mollie's other hand and held it.

When the service was over, Mandie told Celia, "Let's let the crowd get on down ahead of us so we can be sure Mollie doesn't run away somewhere."

Celia agreed. "Yes, it would be bad if she broke away and got lost in all these woods on our way down."

Liza, overhearing the conversation, said, "Missy 'Manda, I needs to go he'p wid de breakfus' or Aunt Lou be lookin' fo' me."

"We're all going to help with the food, Liza. You don't have to hurry," Mandie told her. "I do believe the sun is coming out full force now. Look." She glanced overhead as a gust of wind swept past them.

"It sho' is," Liza agreed. Then she quickly said to Mollie, "Look at dat. Dere be one of dem rainbows I be tellin' you 'bout. Right dere!" She pointed back across the hill.

Mollie turned around to look, and she was so excited she could hardly speak. "Mandie!" she cried, pointing back to the end of the rainbow in the distance. "Mandie! Look!" She began jumping up and down. "Look, Celia, look!"

Mandie stepped back to see the rainbow and immediately exclaimed, "What is that?" She could make out a vague white figure near the end of the rainbow.

Celia squinted as she looked and said, "It's something white."

"Mandie, it's the angel people! Mandie, let's go see!" Mollie said, pulling on her hand.

Liza stared at the figure and said, "Looks more like a ghost to me. And it's supposed to be a pot o' gold at de end of de rainbow, not a ghost!'' She moved closer to Mandie as she shivered.

Mandie quickly decided to investigate. Still holding Mollie's hand and catching one of Liza's hands, she urged them back up the hill with Celia helping on the other side of Mollie. "Come on. Let's go see what it is,'' she said.

Liza tugged at her hand to go the other way, and Mollie pushed ahead. Then when they got closer to the white form, Mandie felt Mollie's footsteps grow slower.

"Come on, now, Mollie, we're going to find out what this is,'' Mandie told her as she continued up the hill and strong gusts of wind blew against them.

As they drew nearer, Mandie could see what looked like a lot of white, fluffy material floating in the air, and then suddenly the top part of it seemed to be broken away by the wind and go flying off into space.

Mandie gasped as she saw carrot-red hair uncovered and the form turned into a woman dressed in all white. The four young people stopped to stare at the woman, and the woman stared at them. Then Mandie came to a quick decision. Practically dragging Mollie with Celia's help, Mandie moved on toward the woman. Finally they were in hearing distance, and when Mandie could see the woman's bright blue eyes, she came to a conclusion.

"You are Mollie's aunt, aren't you?" Mandie asked as they stood face-to-face with the woman. Mollie clung to Mandie's skirt and Liza slipped behind the little girl. Celia stood by, listening and looking.

"That I am,'' the woman said. Then suddenly she came forward and stooped down to get a good look at

Mollie. "And this is my sister's dear little daughter."

Mollie tried to move closer to Mandie, and the woman added, "I am your aunt, child. Come to me." She held her arms out but Mollie didn't budge.

"How did you know where Mollie was?" Mandie asked.

"Ah, that you do not know?" the woman asked. "The detectives hunted and hunted but could not find me because I got married and changed my name. Then weeks and weeks ago, your grandmother, Mrs. Taft, asked your uncle John Shaw to send his man to contact the Cherokee people for help in locating me, and, as you see, they found me."

"Then why didn't you just come to the house instead of hiding out here on the mountain?" Mandie asked.

"My poor sister and I had hard words years ago when I left Ireland, and I was not sure I wanted to see my niece," the woman replied.

"You must have been the one who lured Mollie out of her bed the other night," Celia said.

"Aye, she was," Mollie suddenly spoke.

"And how do you be knowing that?" the woman asked.

"Because ye smell like ye did that night when ye ran off and left me," Mollie told her. "Do ye not want to be me aunt?"

"I am your aunt, dear child. Nothing can change that," the woman said.

"Me name is not child. Me name is Mollie," the little girl replied.

"That I do know, and also your name was spelled wrong on the papers the detectives had," the woman said. "The correct spelling is M-o-l-l-i-e, and they had it spelled M-o-l-l-y, which almost caused me to disclaim any knowledge of you because I thought it was the wrong little girl. So I had to see you for myself. And when I saw that red hair and those blue eyes, I knew you were my sister's child."

"Her name was spelled with a 'y' on the papers the law officers gave my grandmother in Ireland to bring Mollie home with us," Mandie told her. "So I suppose you are going to take Mollie home with you?"

The woman stood up and said, "No, that's impossible right now."

"I want to go back home with Celia," Mollie said.

"Why is it impossible?" Mandie asked, ignoring Mollie's remark.

"Because my husband died three months ago, and I don't have a definite home right now. I am staying with his sister for the time being, but as soon as I can get on my feet again, I will come after Mollie," the woman said.

"Where do you live? What town?" Mandie asked.

"Your uncle John Shaw knows all that," the woman told her. "Now I think it's best I leave since I cannot take Mollie with me." She quickly stooped to kiss Mollie and said, "You be a sweetie, and I will be back for you, soon, I hope."

Mandie saw tears in the woman's eyes as she quickly turned and ran back over the hill, retrieving her white hat from the bushes where it had landed. She disappeared in the distance as the young people watched.

" 'Tweren't no ghost, aftuh all!" Liza said with a big sigh.

"I guess me aunt Lou must've been right. There be

64

no real angel people that we kin see," Mollie said, sadly looking into the distance.

"Aunt Lou is right. There are angels all around but we can't see them," Celia told her.

Mollie looked up at Celia and then at Mandie with tears in her blue eyes and said, "And there be no leprechauns either, no real leprechauns." She shook her head and frowned.

"That's right," Mandie agreed.

Mollie suddenly started to run down the hill. "Let's go tell me grandmither!" she yelled.

Liza ran after her. "I knowed dat all de time," she called to Mollie.

"But it took you both a long time to say it," Mandie said as she and Celia followed.

*Mandie® and Mollie
& the Angel's Visit*

A Drama in Three Acts

by Lois Gladys Leppard

TIME:	1902
PLACE:	Franklin, North Carolina
ACT I:	Scene 1 – The Shaws' parlor. An afternoon in the spring. Scene 2 – The Shaws' kitchen. Same afternoon.
ACT II:	Scene 1 – The Shaws' parlor. After supper on the same day. Scene 2 – The Shaws' parlor. After midnight on the same day.
ACT III:	Scene 1 – On the mountain above Franklin. Sunrise service.

CHARACTERS
(in order of appearance)

Amanda (Mandie) Shaw, thirteen years old, blond hair, blue eyes, small

Celia Hamilton, thirteen years old, auburn hair, green eyes, Mandie's friend

Mollie, ten years old, carrot-red hair, bright blue eyes, Irish orphan

Snowball, Mandie's white cat

Liza, sixteen years old, maid in the Shaw home

Aunt Lou, elderly housekeeper for the Shaw family, large woman

Abraham, elderly handyman for the Shaw family

Jenny, middle-aged cook for the Shaw family, Abraham's wife

Jason Bond, elderly caretaker for John Shaw's businesses, tall, gray hair

Preacher, elderly man, tall, heavyset

The Woman, in her thirties, Mollie's aunt from Ireland, carrot-red hair, blue eyes

Audience on mountain for service

ACT I—Scene 1

THE SCENE: *The parlor in the Shaws' house. Two large windows upstage show the porch outside. Open draperies are on them. A table with an oil lamp is in front of one window and a chair is in front of the other. To the left is a large fireplace with chairs in front of it. A settee sits at the right near a door into the hallway. A stool is nearby. It is the afternoon.*

AT CURTAIN: *The stage is empty. The door is already open, and Mandie enters with her friend, Celia, and the little orphan girl, Mollie.*

MANDIE

(*Walking over to the settee and sitting down.*)

Celia, I'm so glad you and your mother could come and spend the Easter holidays with us. And could bring Mollie, too. I do believe she has grown a couple of inches since we brought her home with us from Ireland.

(*Mandie looks at Mollie, who is wandering about the room.*)

CELIA

(*Sitting on the settee next to Mandie.*)

She is growing fast. And she also gets around fast, you'll find out.

MOLLIE

(*After inspecting everything in the room, she comes to stand in front of the fireplace.*)

Mandie, do ye be havin' leprechauns in this place where ye live?

(*She frowns and pushes back a lock of hair as she looks at Mandie.*)

MANDIE

(*She sighs.*)

Oh, Mollie, are you still chasing leprechauns? I don't believe we have any in this house, or in this town, in fact.

MOLLIE

(*Walking closer to look at Mandie.*)

But there might be one here someplace. I'll be lookin' and watchin' for one while I be stayin' here with ye.

MANDIE

But you don't need to find one now to get his pot of gold. You have a nice home with Celia.

MOLLIE

When Celia finds me aunt, the lady may be needin' the gold.

CELIA

We may never find your aunt, Mollie. So far the detectives my mother has had looking for her haven't found any trace of her, so you may have to live with us until you grow up.

MOLLIE

(*Looking at Celia thoughtfully.*)

I still be lookin' for a leprechaun.

> (*Snowball, Mandie's white cat, wanders into the room.*)

MOLLIE

(*Picking up Snowball and going to sit on the stool.*)

I know ye. Yer name be Snowball, and ye came to Ireland with Mandie last summer.

MANDIE

(*In a low voice to Celia.*)

Is your mother still trying to find Mollie's aunt, or has she given up?

CELIA

(*In a low voice.*)

No, she hasn't given up, but so far no one has found a trace of her. Remember the police authorities in Ireland told your grandmother that the aunt had come to the United States when Mollie was a baby. That's a long time ago.

MANDIE

But they also told us that the aunt was last heard from somewhere in Virginia. Of course she might have moved on to another part of the country.

(*Lowering her voice to a whisper.*)

Does your mother plan to keep her if she never locates the aunt?

CELIA

(*In a whisper.*)

I think so. She is quite a handful, never having had any discipline in Ireland and being allowed to roam the streets there, but Aunt Rebecca has become attached to her, and I sorta think she hopes we never find her aunt so she can keep Mollie.

MANDIE

How is your aunt Rebecca doing in trying to educate her?

CELIA

(*With a big smile.*)

Well, you know Aunt Rebecca used to be a school-teacher, and this gives her something to do.

MANDIE

Have y'all heard anything more about Mrs. Wiley, the woman who was keeping Mollie in Ireland?

CELIA

Yes, Mother stays in touch with her. I'm sure Mother sends her money, too. The woman is still in such bad shape—after that accident she had and no one to support her. Even though she is in that rest home for the poor in Belfast, she does need some money.

MANDIE

(*Rubbing her arms.*)

It still gives me goose bumps just thinking about that awful fire. I'm so thankful we were able to save Mollie and Mrs. Wiley, although the lady did get seriously injured.

CELIA

I know. Never in all my thirteen years have I been so frightened.

LIZA

(*Appearing in the doorway and standing there to look into the room.*)

MANDIE

(*Seeing Liza.*)

Come on in, Liza. This is Mollie. (*She motions toward Mollie.*) And, Mollie, this is Liza.

MOLLIE

(*Jumping up and running to stand in front of Liza. She drops the cat in her haste. Snowball runs out the door.*)

Do ye be knowin' if there be leprechauns in this house?

LIZA

(*Frowning as she looks at Mollie and then at Mandie.*)

Be whut? Missy 'Manda, dat lil' girl she don't speak good English.

MANDIE

(*Smiling.*)

She wants to know if we have leprechauns in this house.

LIZA

(*Looking puzzled.*)

If we has whut?

MANDIE

Leprechauns. You have probably never heard of leprechauns. You see, some people in Ireland believe they exist. And Mollie is always looking for one because they are supposed to own a pot of gold.

LIZA

(*Her eyes widening.*)

Pot o' gold?

CELIA

(*Looking at Mandie.*)

You might as well explain what this is all about.

MANDIE

Yes. Many, many years ago, Liza, these leprechauns were supposed to live in Ireland. The English or American name for them is shoemaker—

LIZA

(*Excitedly interrupting.*)

Like dat shoemaker man named Pat whut works down in dat shop on Main Street? But he ain't got no pot o' gold.

MOLLIE

(*Becoming excited.*)

Ye know where there be a leprechaun? Show me where he be.

MANDIE

(*Loudly.*)

No, Liza, Pat is a shoemaker, but he's not a leprechaun. Maybe leprechauns only lived in Ireland. We don't have any here.

MOLLIE

(*Grasping Liza's hand.*)

Will ye take me to see this Pat shoemaker? Please, I say.

LIZA

(*Looking from Mollie to Mandie and then back to Mollie.*)

But Missy 'Manda she say dis heah Pat he ain't de right kind o' lepcawn, or whatever you calls it. And he sho ain't got no pot o' gold. Now iffen dat's all you lookin' fo', why don't you find de end to de rainbow? Dey say it's a pot o' gold at de end.

MOLLIE

Do ye be knowin' where this rainbow be?

MANDIE

(*Speaking sharply to Liza.*)

Liza! Please don't put such nonsensical ideas into Mollie's head. You know very well there is no pot of gold at the end of the rainbow, which I know you must have learned in church.

LIZA

I knows.

MANDIE

(*Looking at Mollie.*)

The rainbow is God's promise to us, all of us here on earth, that the earth will never again be destroyed by water. He gave the promise to Noah after the flood was over.

MOLLIE

(*Looking at Mandie in surprise.*)

But how do ye be knowin' all this?

MANDIE

Because it's all in the Bible.

(*Looking at Celia.*)

Y'all have been teaching her the Bible, haven't you?

CELIA

Of course, Mandie. But there is so much she doesn't know that it's going to take a lot of time for her to understand everything.

MOLLIE

(*Looking at Liza.*)

Anyhow, kin we find a rainbow?

LIZA

Missy 'Manda, she be right 'bout rainbows. Ain't no pot o' gold at de end. Dat's jes' ole tales.

(*Looking at Mandie.*)

I'se sorry fo' all de tomfoolery, Missy 'Manda. 'Course I knows bettuh. Aunt Lou she tell me all 'bout rainbows long time ago.

MOLLIE

(*Quickly pulling on Liza's arm to get her attention.*)

Kin we find a rainbow? Please, I say.

MANDIE

(*Looking at Liza.*)

You are forgiven this time, Liza, but please remember that Mollie is young and doesn't know everything you've been taught. In fact, you could help us teach her what Easter is all about while she's here.

LIZA

(*Looking at Mandie with widened eyes.*)

Missy 'Manda, I don't be knowin' how to teach nobody nuthin'. Y'all be needin' Aunt Lou to do de teachin'.

MANDIE

(*Smiling at Liza.*)

That's a good idea, Liza. We'll ask Aunt Lou to help explain things to Mollie.

MOLLIE

(*Suddenly, loudly, looking up at Liza.*)

Kin we find a rainbow? Kin we?

(*Then she looks at Mandie.*)

MANDIE

All right, Mollie, if a rainbow comes into the sky while you are here, we'll be sure to show it to you. You see, we can't just make rainbows whenever we want one. God puts them in the sky, usually when the sun comes out after it rains.

MOLLIE

We kin look for leprechauns then. Maybe they don't be made by God.

CELIA

Mollie, God made this earth and everything in it. So if there is such a thing as a leprechaun, I'm sure God made it, too. However, I don't believe He made any leprechauns, because if He did, sooner or later you'd be able to find one.

MOLLIE

(*Frowning and stomping both her feet.*)

Then I be wantin' to go back to Ireland, where God didn't make everythin'.

LIZA

(*Quickly turning to leave the room.*)

And I'se got to go back to de kitchen 'fo Aunt Lou start lookin' fo' me.

(*Liza exits through the doorway.*)

(*Mandie and Celia look at each other in dismay.*)

CELIA

So far only Aunt Rebecca has been able to get through to her.

MOLLIE

(*Suddenly sitting down on the floor near the door.*)

Where be Grandmither? She took me to this United States. Now I be wantin' Grandmither to take me back to Belfast. That I do.

MANDIE

(*Quickly slipping out of her seat and sitting on the floor next to Mollie. She puts an arm around Mollie.*)

Grandmother will be coming later this week, but we don't want her to take you back to Ireland. Remember the cold place in the cellar where you lived? And lots of times you didn't have enough to eat. We want you to stay in the United States so we can take care of you, at least until we can locate your aunt.

(*Reaching to smooth Mollie's hair.*)

MOLLIE

(*Pulling away from Mandie.*)

But I might be findin' a leprechaun in Ireland, and then I could git his pot o' gold, and I could be gittin' me a new home to stay in, that I could.

CELIA

(*Coming to sit on the floor with Mandie and Mollie.*)

Mollie, have you ever thought about the fact that if you did find a leprechaun and he had a pot of gold, you couldn't take the gold away from him because it would belong to him? That wouldn't be nice to take something away from someone that it belonged to.

MOLLIE

(*Looking at Celia for a moment.*)

But he would be knowin' where he could be findin' another pot o' gold. That he would.

CELIA

But suppose he had to work many long years and save to fill that pot with gold, like you had to work for your food when you lived in Ireland?

MOLLIE

(*After a pause.*)

Where be that Indian uncle? He helped me look for leprechauns in Ireland, that he did.

MANDIE

Uncle Ned. He's not actually my uncle. He was my father's Cherokee friend. He and his family will probably meet up with us on the mountain at sunrise on Sunday.

MOLLIE

On the mountain? Sunrise?

MANDIE

Yes, we will be going up the mountain Sunday to see the sun rise and to hear the Easter sermon.

MOLLIE

(*Looking at Mandie and then at Celia.*)

Then kin we look for leprechauns on the mountain?

MANDIE

There aren't any leprechauns on the mountain. We'll find something else to do up there. We'll sing.

MOLLIE

Sing? And kin we dance, too?

MANDIE

(*Becoming impatient.*)

No, Mollie, we will not dance. Easter is a special holy day. We'll be celebrating the time that Jesus rose from His tomb.

MOLLIE

Celebratin'? Will we be havin' a party? Like a birthday party?

MANDIE

(*Standing up and looking at Celia.*)

Let's take this child to Aunt Lou and ask her to explain a few things. I don't seem to be getting anywhere with it myself.

CELIA

(*Smiling as she also rises.*)

You are doing better than I have been able to do. But Aunt Lou sounds like the perfect teacher.

MANDIE

(*Reaching for Mollie's hand.*)

Come on, Mollie, we want you to meet Aunt Lou. You'll

love her, I'm sure. She's in charge of everything here—cooking the food, sewing clothes, and running everything.

(*Mollie stands up.*)

(*Mandie leads her toward the door. Celia follows.*)

CURTAIN

ACT I—Scene 2

THE SCENE: *The kitchen in the Shaws' house. Two windows upstage center near an iron cookstove, woodbox beside it. A sink to the left upstage. A long table with several chairs stands near center stage. Door to right. Same afternoon.*

AT CURTAIN: *Aunt Lou is standing in the middle of the floor supervising Liza and Jenny the cook as they prepare food on the stove. Abraham is arranging wood in the woodbox. They all stop to look as Mandie, Celia, and Mollie enter through the door at the right. Snowball follows.*

AUNT LOU

(*Walking toward Mollie with her arms out to hug her.*)

Here's dat lil' angel from Ireland.

MOLLIE

(*Frowning at her.*)

I don't be no angel. Mollie I be.

AUNT LOU

(*Bending down to look at her.*)

I knows you ain't no real angel. Come to Aunt Lou.

MOLLIE

(*Allowing Aunt Lou to embrace her.*)

Will you be me aunt? Celia and her mither they look and look for me aunt and don't find her. Will you be me aunt?

(*Looking up into Aunt Lou's smiling face.*)

AUNT LOU

'Course I'll be yo' aunt. Now you jes' call me Aunt Lou and I'll be proud to be yo' aunt.

MOLLIE

(*Staring at Aunt Lou.*)

Do ye be needin' a pot o' gold then?

AUNT LOU

(*Glancing at Mandie with a puzzled look.*)

A pot of gold? Now whut would I do wid a pot of gold? I don't need no gold.

MOLLIE

(*Looking at Mandie.*)

Then I don't be havin' to take his pot o' gold when I find a leprechaun.

(*Aunt Lou straightens up to look at Mandie.*)

(*Mollie holds on to Aunt Lou's big white apron.*)

MANDIE

Oh, Aunt Lou, it's all so confusing. Mollie needs a teacher, and I think you'd be better at that than I am. She just doesn't understand anything I try to explain. Please say you'll help.

AUNT LOU

Liza done told me whut was said in de parlor a while ago. I'll see whut I kin do. Aftuh while, dat is. Right now we'se got to git supper done.

(*Turning to Mollie and patting Mollie's head.*)

Now I'll be yo' aunt, but you's got to go back to de parlor so I kin git dis heah food cooked, you heah?

MOLLIE

(*Looking up at Aunt Lou as she pulls on Aunt Lou's apron.*)

If I be goin' back to the parlor, ye won't go 'way some place, will ye? Will ye, I say?

AUNT LOU

No, no, I won't be goin' no place. (*She pulls her apron out of Mollie's hand.*) I stays right heah in dis kitchen till I gits de supper on de table so you kin eat. Ain't you hungry now?

(*Moving toward the stove.*)

MOLLIE

I may be a little hungry. What do ye be wantin' me to do to pay fer it?

AUNT LOU

I be wantin' you to go back to de parlor now.

MANDIE

Aunt Lou, she hasn't met everyone else.

(*Taking Mollie by the hand, she leads her over to Jenny and Abraham, who have been listening.*)

Mollie, this is Jenny and her husband, Abraham. And you already know Liza over there.

ABRAHAM

Howdy, little missy.

JENNY

And you come all de way 'cross dat big ocean from Ireland.

MOLLIE

No, I come from Virginny with Celia and her mither. Before that I be in Ireland.

ABRAHAM

Ireland, where dey has leprechauns.

MANDIE

(*Taking a quick breath.*)

Abraham, please don't mention the word.

MOLLIE

(*Her blue eyes open wide.*)

Leprechauns, ye say.

(*Leaning toward Abraham she whispers.*)

Do ye be havin' leprechauns here, I say?

MANDIE

(*Rolling her eyes and shaking her head behind Mollie's back and whispering.*)

No.

ABRAHAM

(*Quickly to Mollie.*)

Ain't no sech thing as leprechauns in dis heah place. Only find dem in Ireland.

MANDIE

(*Under her breath.*)

Oh no!

MOLLIE

(*Moving closer to Abraham.*)

Will ye go to Ireland with me and hunt for leprechauns then? Will ye, I say?

ABRAHAM

(*Looking at Mandie as he quickly walks toward the back door.*)

One o' dese days we'll do jes' dat. Right now I has to git de wood fo' de stove.

(*He exits through the door.*)

MOLLIE

(*Calling after Abraham.*)

One day soon we be goin' to Ireland then.

(*Picking up Snowball, who has been sitting nearby.*)

MANDIE

Come on, Mollie, we have to go back to the parlor so all these people can get supper done.

(*Mandie walks toward the door.*)

(*Mollie, holding the cat, follows her.*)

CELIA

(*Following Mandie.*)

I can see where we're going to have some interesting holidays this week.

MANDIE

I'm hoping Aunt Lou can make her understand what the holidays are all about.

CURTAIN

ACT II—Scene 1

THE SCENE: *Same day, after supper. In the Shaws'*
parlor. The lamp is lit on the table by the
window. It is dark outside, seen through
the window.

AT CURTAIN: *Mandie and Celia are sitting on the settee*
talking.

MANDIE

I wonder what kind of an errand Uncle John sent Mr.
Jason on tonight. I heard them talking in the hallway
after supper, and when they saw me they just shut up.

CELIA

It's probably about some of your uncle's business matters that don't concern anyone else.

MANDIE

I'd still like to know where he sent him.

> (*Mollie comes running into the parlor. Aunt Lou*
> *walks in behind her, carrying a Bible.*)

MOLLIE

> (*Excitedly she comes to stand in front of Mandie*
> *and Celia.*)

Me aunt Lou has been readin' a good book to me. It be all about these people called angels. They be like leprechauns. Not everybody kin see them.

AUNT LOU

(*Shaking her head as she looks at Mandie.*)

I'll keep tryin', my chile. Mebbe sumthin' will soak in after a while. Now I'm plumb wore out and I'm going to git some rest. Good night.

MANDIE

Thanks, Aunt Lou. Good night.

(*Aunt Lou exits out the back door.*)

MOLLIE

(*Still standing before Mandie and Celia.*)

The angel people are all white, me aunt thinks. And sometimes they do good things, but there be one bad one that God didn't like, and He threw him all the way down to where the Devil be. And he can't iver come back to live with the good angel people because he's been bad. But me aunt Lou thinks God won't throw us down there for being bad if we be sorry. So when I be bad, all I have to do is be sorry, and I always be sorry when I be bad. Do ye be sorry when ye be bad, Mandie? Do ye, Celia? Do ye?

CELIA

Of course I am, Mollie.

MANDIE

(*Smiling at Mollie.*)

Yes, I'm always sorry for being bad, but I try real hard not to be bad. And I always ask God to forgive me.

MOLLIE

Me aunt Lou said she would show me how to talk to God tomorrow when she reads me more of that book, because I don't be knowin' how to ask God to forgive me when I've been bad, and I need to know real soon just in case I be bad agin.

CELIA

Oh, Mollie, I'm sure Aunt Lou will be able to teach you about God.

(*Snowball comes running into the room and goes to sit on the hearth.*)

MOLLIE

(*Watching the cat.*)

Mandie, do ye be thinkin' Snowball might be a angel cat? He do be white.

MANDIE

(*Smiling.*)

No, Mollie, he's just a real live white cat.

MOLLIE

(*Sitting down on the floor.*)

I think me tired.

MANDIE

And I think it's bedtime. I'm going to let you sleep with me tonight, Mollie, since you are in a strange house.

MOLLIE

(*Frowning.*)

This be a strange house?

MANDIE

It's a different house from the one you've been living in, and you never have been here before, so I thought you might like to sleep with me.

MOLLIE

No, no, Mandie. I be wantin' a whole big bed all by me-self.

MANDIE

Then we will put you in the room next to mine. It has a door between, so if you change your mind you can always come in my room and get in the bed with me.

MOLLIE

(*Shaking her head.*)

Oh, Mandie, 'tis afraid ye be thinkin' I be. I sleep in a big bed by meself at Celia's house, and I don't be afraid.

CELIA

She's definitely not afraid of the dark. She gets up sometimes in the middle of the night and wanders all over the house.

MANDIE

(*Looking at Mollie.*)

That's not allowed here, Mollie. You would wake people up if you go roaming around during the night, and I don't think anybody would like that.

MOLLIE

(*Yawning.*)

I do be sleepy.

MANDIE

(*Rising.*)

All right, Mollie, we are going to bed. I believe everybody else has already done that. Come on.

> (*Celia rises and reaches a hand down to pull Mollie to her feet.*)

MOLLIE

(*Quickly standing up.*)

I not be asleep yit, Celia.

MANDIE

Off to bed we go.

(*Mandie, Celia, and Mollie exit through the door.*)

CURTAIN

ACT II—Scene 2

THE SCENE: *Later that night, after midnight. In the Shaws' parlor. It is dark.*

AT CURTAIN: *Mandie enters with a lighted lamp that illuminates the room. Celia comes in behind her through the door.*

MANDIE

(*Setting the lamp on the table and standing by the table.*)

I just can't imagine where Mollie could be. We've searched everywhere, and she's just not here.

CELIA

(*Coming to stand by the table.*)

I told you she gets up in the middle of the night and wanders all over the house. There's no way to stop her that we can figure out.

MANDIE

Where does she go? Where do you find her?

CELIA

She does all kinds of things. Sometimes we find her eating food out of the icebox, and sometimes she's curled up asleep in the parlor. We never know where to look for her.

MANDIE

Does she ever go outdoors?

CELIA

Not that we know of. But, Mandie, she couldn't be outdoors right now because all the doors are locked.

> (*There is a loud metallic click and the sound of squeaky hinges.*)

MANDIE

> (*Looking at Celia.*)

What was that?

CELIA

> (*Moving closer to Mandie.*)

Someone is coming in the front door.

MANDIE

Can't be Mollie. Whoever it is has a key.

> (*Jason Bond suddenly looks into the parlor through the doorway.*)

JASON BOND

Just looking to see who had the lamp lit, whether I should put it out for the night.

MANDIE

(*Blowing out her breath.*)

Oh, Mr. Jason, thank goodness it's you.

JASON BOND

What are you two doing down here this time of night?

MANDIE

We're looking for Mollie. She's not in her bedroom. But where have you been this time of night, Mr. Jason?

JASON BOND

On an errand for your uncle. Now we probably ought to find that little girl. I'll help y'all look for her.

MANDIE

We've already searched everywhere we can think of and we can't find her.

JASON BOND

I'll help y'all look, but let me just go to the kitchen first and get a bite to eat since I missed supper last night. I'll be right back.

(*Jason Bond exits through the door.*)

MANDIE

(*Calling to Mr. Bond as she goes to sit on the settee.*)

I'll be here.

CELIA

(*Sitting beside Mandie.*)

So will I.

(*Snowball comes into the room and Mandie picks him up in her lap.*)

MANDIE

I'm hoping Mr. Jason will tell us where he's been.

CELIA

Mandie, I don't think he's going to tell us a single thing. He didn't explain anything when he told us he had been on an errand.

(*Snowball suddenly jumps down from Mandie's lap.*)

MANDIE

Snowball, where are you going?

(*As she watches him run across the floor, she happens to look at the window.*)

Celia, look, look!

(*Mandie rises and hurries over to the window.*)

CELIA

(*Following Mandie.*)

Mandie, what is it?

MANDIE

(*As she reaches the window, she points through the glass.*)

There's Mollie! She must have gone out through this window. See, she's trying to open it and get back in. I'll let her in through the front door.

(*Celia continues to look through the window.*)

(*Mandie exits through the door to the hallway and can be heard offstage. There is the sound of a door being opened.*)

MANDIE

(*Offstage.*)

Mollie, get in this house! Where have you been?

(*Sound offstage of door being closed.*)

(*Mollie rushes into the parlor through the door.*)

(*Mandie follows.*)

MANDIE

Mollie, you didn't answer me. Where have you been?

MOLLIE

(*Going to stand near Celia.*)

I be seein' one of them angel people like me aunt Lou told me about. Me aunt Lou was right. They do be angel people, all white like she be sayin'. The angel people kin talk, too. But the angel people flew away while I be watchin'. All white and—

MANDIE

(*Grasping Mollie's hand and leading her to the settee, where she sits down and pulls Mollie up beside her.*)

Mollie, please be quiet a minute. I want to ask you some questions.

CELIA

(*Sitting next to them on the settee.*)

Yes, we do.

MOLLIE

(*Jerking her hand out of Mandie's.*)

I be quiet if'n ye don't be squeezin' me hand.

(*Flexing her fingers and pretending to be hurt.*)

MANDIE

(*Quickly reaching to kiss Mollie's hand.*)

I'm sorry, Mollie. I didn't mean to hurt you. Now let's begin at the beginning. Where have you been? We've looked the house over for you, and it's the middle of the night. We all need to be in bed and asleep.

MOLLIE

(*Looking up at Mandie.*)

But, Mandie, I was in the bed, but this angel people—I really be sure it was a leprechaun angel, that it was—it came to me bed and asked me to follow it. So I—

CELIA

You must have been dreaming, Mollie. The house was all locked up and nobody could get in.

MOLLIE

Oh, but mistaken ye be. All the doors was locked, but this leprechaun angel showed me the way to that window over there. It was open, it was. And it says to me real softlike, ''follow, follow,'' and I follow. I be thinkin' this leprechaun angel may be takin' me to its pot o' gold, so I go out the window—

CELIA

Where did you go when you went out the window, Mollie?

107

MOLLIE

There be a house back there with horses in it, there is. I be followin' this leprechaun angel, and it went into this house, and I followed just like it told me, but then I couldn't find it, I couldn't. It went plumb away, bless Pat, plumb away, gone.

(*Mollie shakes her head sadly.*)

MANDIE

You were gone a long time, Mollie, because we have been searching the whole house for you and that took time.

MOLLIE

I be gone a long time because I be lookin' to find the leprechaun angel, but that I could not do. I looked and looked and looked, in all the bushes and behind all the trees, but it went away, it did.

MANDIE

(*Watching Mollie's face.*)

What did this thing, or person, look like? Was it tall or short? A man or a woman? Did it say anything else to you?

MOLLIE

It was tall, taller than ye, Mandie. But I don't be knowin' what it might be lookin' like 'cause it didn't have a face.

It was all covered up with white linen just like me mither made in Belfast Mill.

CELIA

Did it talk?

MOLLIE

It said nary a word to me but "follow, follow," and so I followed, but it floated away, sure it did, and I looked and looked, and I could not find it. Why do ye be supposin' it told me to follow it and then it would not let me find it agin?

(*She looks puzzled.*)

JASON BOND

(*Entering through the door to the hall.*)

So you found her, did you?

MANDIE

No, not exactly. She had gone out through that window over there and was trying to get back inside, and we saw her.

JASON BOND

At least she's back, safe and sound.

(*Lowering his voice.*)

You might try turning the key, you know, tonight.

(*Making a motion to indicate locking the door.*)

MANDIE

If I can figure out how to do that without a loud protest.

JASON BOND

Well, I believe it's time for me to get a little sleep. Gotta get up early again in the morning.

(*Starts toward the door.*)

MANDIE

Mr. Jason, do you have to go on another errand for my uncle?

JASON BOND

(*Stopping to look back at Mandie.*)

Now you know your uncle's business is confidential and I can't discuss it with anyone, so I think you shouldn't worry your pretty little head over such things. And I also think you girls, all three of you, should crawl back in your beds and get some sleep. Otherwise y'all are going to be awfully sleepyheaded tomorrow. Night, night now.

(*Jason Bond exits through the door to the hall.*)

MANDIE

(*Rising from the settee.*)

Guess we might as well. Come on, Mollie. We're all going back to bed.

MOLLIE

(*Standing up.*)

Are ye sure we must go to bed?

MANDIE

Yes, I am sure.

CELIA

And this time, Mollie, you must stay in your bed for the rest of the night.

MOLLIE

But what if the leprechaun angel comes back to see me and wants me to follow it?

MANDIE

Mollie, there is no such thing as a leprechaun angel.

MOLLIE

But, Mandie, I just told ye I saw one.

(*Mollie follows Mandie to the door. Celia follows her.*)

111

MANDIE

We'll talk about that tomorrow. Right now we are all going to bed, and we are going to stay in our beds until it's time to get up for breakfast.

CELIA

(*Stopping to point back to the lighted lamp.*)

Do you want to leave it here?

MANDIE

(*Turning back and going toward the lamp.*)

Y'all go ahead. I'll put the lamp out.

(*Celia and Mollie exit through the door.*)
(*Mandie walks over to the lamp on the table and blows out the light. She starts to turn and leave the room when she quickly looks back out the window.*)

MANDIE

(*To herself.*)

What was that?

(*She leans near the window to look outside.*)

I thought I saw something out there.

(*She keeps staring out the window and finally turns to leave the room.*)

112

I must be imagining things after all the excitement to-night. There's no such thing as a leprechaun angel. Bunch of malarkey!

CURTAIN

ACT III—Scene 1

THE SCENE: *Easter Sunday sunrise service on the mountain above Franklin. The sun will rise and brighten the scene as the preacher gives the message.*

AT CURTAIN: *The preacher is standing upstage center, elevated a little above the crowd that stands before him. Mandie, Celia, Liza, and Mollie are downstage center.*

PREACHER

I'm happy to see so many wonderful people made it out of bed and up the mountain this morning to give thanks to our Lord for this special day. Let us pray.

(The preacher watches to see that heads are bowed. Then he begins his prayer.)

We thank Thee, Dear God, for this glorious morning and for what it stands for. We thank Thee for clearing away the rain we had last night so that we may be able to see the sun rise this morning. Now we offer our thanks up to you in song.

MOLLIE

(Excitedly speaking, overlapping the last few words of the preacher.)

115

There's the angel people, Mandie! Look!

(*She points to upstage right.*)

MANDIE

(*Bending to whisper to Mollie.*)

Sh-h-h-h! Be quiet!

MOLLIE

But, Mandie—

MANDIE

Sh-h-h-h-h! Hush!

(*The crowd had begun singing "He Is Risen," and Mandie, Celia, and Liza join in.*)

(*Mollie tries to see through the crowd in the direction she had pointed about the angel people.*)

PREACHER

(*After the end of the song.*)

Now may the Lord go with you forevermore, my brethren. God bless you all.

(*The crowd starts to break up and go back down the mountain, to the right.*)

MANDIE

(*Looking at Celia and quickly grasping Mollie's hand.*)

116

Let's let the crowd get on down ahead of us so we can be sure Mollie doesn't run away somewhere.

CELIA

Yes, it would be bad if she broke away and got lost in all these woods on our way down.

LIZA

(*Listening to the conversation.*)

I needs to go he'p wid de breakfus', Missy 'Manda, or Aunt Lou be lookin' fo' me.

MANDIE

We're all going to help with the food, Liza. You don't have to hurry.

(*Glancing overhead as a strong gust of wind sweeps past them.*)

I do believe the sun is coming out full force now. Look.

(*Pointing toward the sun.*)

LIZA

(*Looking at the sky.*)

It sho' is.

(*Turning to Mollie.*)

Look at dat. Dere be one of dem rainbows I be tellin' you 'bout. Right dere!

(*She points back across the hill.*)

MOLLIE

(*Turning to look and becoming excited as she points toward the rainbow and jumps up and down.*)

Mandie, look! Look, Celia, look!

MANDIE

(*Stepping back to look at the rainbow. She sees something near it and exclaims.*)

What is that?

MOLLIE

(*Pulling on Mandie's hand.*)

Mandie, it's the angel people! Mandie, let's go see!

CELIA

It's something white.

LIZA

(*Moving closer to Mandie as she shivers.*)

Looks like a ghost to me. And it's supposed to be a pot o' gold at de end of de rainbow, not a ghost!

MANDIE

(*Still holding Mollie's hand as she leads the way with Celia and Liza following her and Mollie.*)

Come on. Let's go see what it is. Looks like a lot of white, fluffy material floating in the air.

(*As they get nearer, the top part of the white form seems to break away and go flying off into the air with a strong gust of wind, uncovering the head of a woman with carrot-red hair.*)

LIZA

(*Grasping Mandie's other hand.*)

It broke!

MOLLIE

I thought it be the angel people.

(*She tries to pull back.*)

MANDIE

(*Pulling on Mollie's hand as they come closer to the woman.*)

You are Mollie's aunt, aren't you?

CELIA

(*Stopping to look at the woman.*)

She has to be with that red hair.

THE WOMAN

(*Coming forward and stooping down to get a look at Mollie, who is trying to hide behind Mandie's skirt.*)

That I am. And this is my sister's dear daughter. I am your aunt, child. Come to me.

MANDIE

How did you know where Mollie was?

THE WOMAN

(*Still stooping and looking up at Mandie.*)

Ah, that you do not know? The detectives hunted and hunted but could not find me because I got married and changed my name. Then weeks and weeks ago, your grandmother, Mrs. Taft, asked your uncle John Shaw to send his man to contact the Cherokee people to help locate me, and, as you see, they found me.

MANDIE

Then why didn't you just come to the house instead of hiding out here on the mountain?

THE WOMAN

My poor sister and I had hard words years ago when I left Ireland, and I was not sure I wanted to see my niece.

CELIA

You must have been the one who lured Mollie out of her bed the other night.

MOLLIE

Aye, she was.

THE WOMAN

And how do you be knowin' that, child?

MOLLIE

Because ye smell like ye did that night when ye ran off and left me.

(*Taking a deep breath and blowing it out.*)

Do ye not want to be me aunt?

THE WOMAN

I am your aunt, dear child. Nothing can change that.

MOLLIE

Me name is not child. Me name is Mollie.

THE WOMAN

That I do know, and also your name was spelled wrong on the papers the detectives had. The correct spelling is M-o-l-l-i-e, and they had it spelled M-o-l-l-y, which almost caused me to disclaim any knowledge of you because I thought it was the wrong little girl, so I had to see you for myself. And when I saw that red hair and blue eyes, I knew you were my sister's child.

MANDIE

Her name was spelled with a 'y' on the papers the law officers gave my grandmother in Ireland to bring Mollie home with us. So I suppose you are going to take Mollie home with you?

MOLLIE

I want to go back home with Celia.

THE WOMAN

(*Standing up.*)

No, that's impossible for me to take her with me right now.

MANDIE

Why is it impossible?

THE WOMAN

Because my husband died three months ago, and I don't have a definite home right now. I am staying with his sister for the time being, but as soon as I can get on my feet again, I will come after Mollie.

MANDIE

Where do you live? What town?

THE WOMAN

Your uncle John Shaw knows all that. Now I think it's best I leave since I cannot take Mollie with me.

(*Stooping to quickly kiss Mollie.*)

You be a sweetie, and I will be back for you, soon I hope.

(*Her voice quivers with emotion.*)

(*As the young people watch, the woman runs back over the hill, retrieves her hat from the bushes where it had landed, and disappears in the distance.*)

LIZA

(*Grinning.*)

'Tweren't no ghost aftuh all!

MOLLIE

(*Looking into the distance.*)

I guess me aunt Lou must've been right. There be no real angel people that we kin see.

MANDIE

Aunt Lou is right. There are angels all around but we can't see them.

MOLLIE

(*Looking up at Mandie and then at Celia and then at Liza.*)

And there be no leprechauns either, no real leprechauns.

(*She shakes her head and frowns.*)

CELIA

That's right.

MOLLIE

(*Suddenly starts to run down the hill.*)

Let's go and tell me grandmither.

LIZA

(*Running after Mollie.*)

I knowed dat all de time.

MANDIE

(*Following.*)

But it sure took you both a long time to say it.

(*Celia follows.*)

CURTAIN